Disney · PIXAR
MONSTERS
UNIVERSITY

PaRragon

Bath · New York · Cologne · Melbourne · Delhi
Hong Kong · Shenzhen · Singapore · Amsterdam

When Mike Wazowski was six years old, he went on a field trip to Monsters, Inc. He snuck inside a child's bedroom and saw a Scarer at work. That one amazing moment made Mike realize he wanted to be a Scarer himself when he grew up!

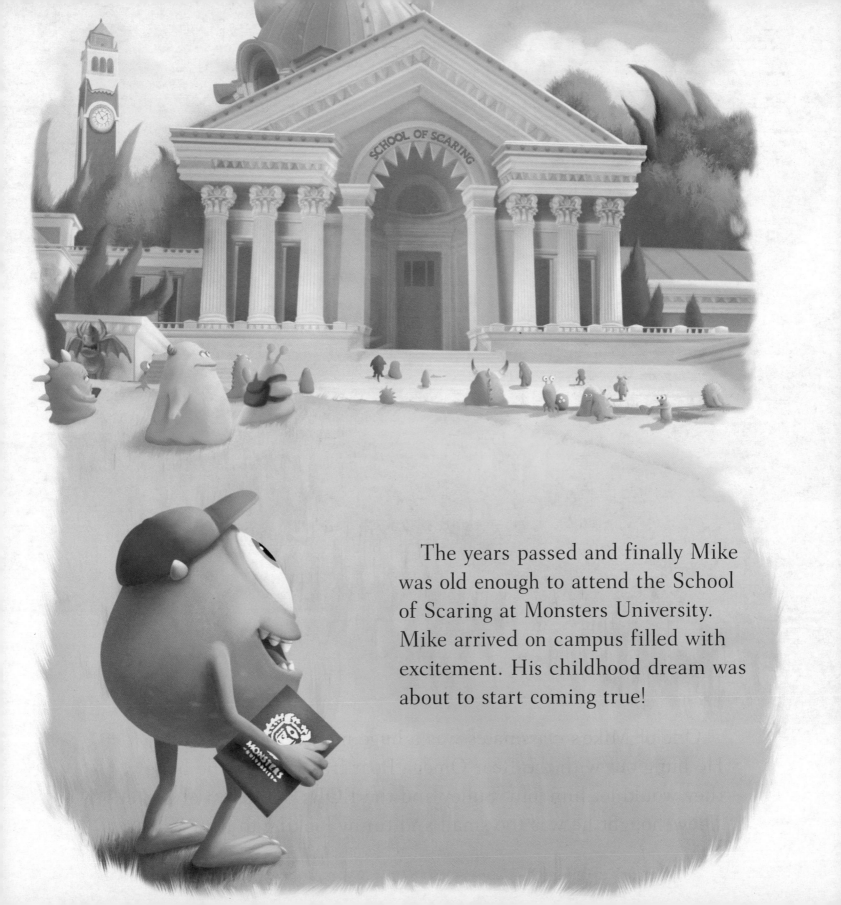

The years passed and finally Mike was old enough to attend the School of Scaring at Monsters University. Mike arrived on campus filled with excitement. His childhood dream was about to start coming true!

One of Mike's classmates was a huge monster named Sulley.
He hung out with the Roar Omega Roar fraternity in the hope
they would let him join. Sulley and the RORs made fun of Mike.
They thought he was too small and funny looking to be a Scarer.

Mike was determined to study hard and ace his final exam. Meanwhile, all Sulley did was mess around. He thought that being big and having a loud roar were enough to make him the best Scarer.

During the final exam, Mike and Sulley got
into a terrible fight. They accidentally broke
Dean Hardscrabble's prized scream can.
As punishment, she decided that neither of them
would continue in the Scaring Programme!

Winning the annual Scare Games was Mike and Sulley's only way of getting back into the Scaring Programme. To compete in the games, they had to join a fraternity. They joined the least scary group on campus: Oozma Kappa. The members of OK were Don, Art, Squishy, and Terri and Terry.

Mike wasn't happy about working with Sulley – but he had no choice.

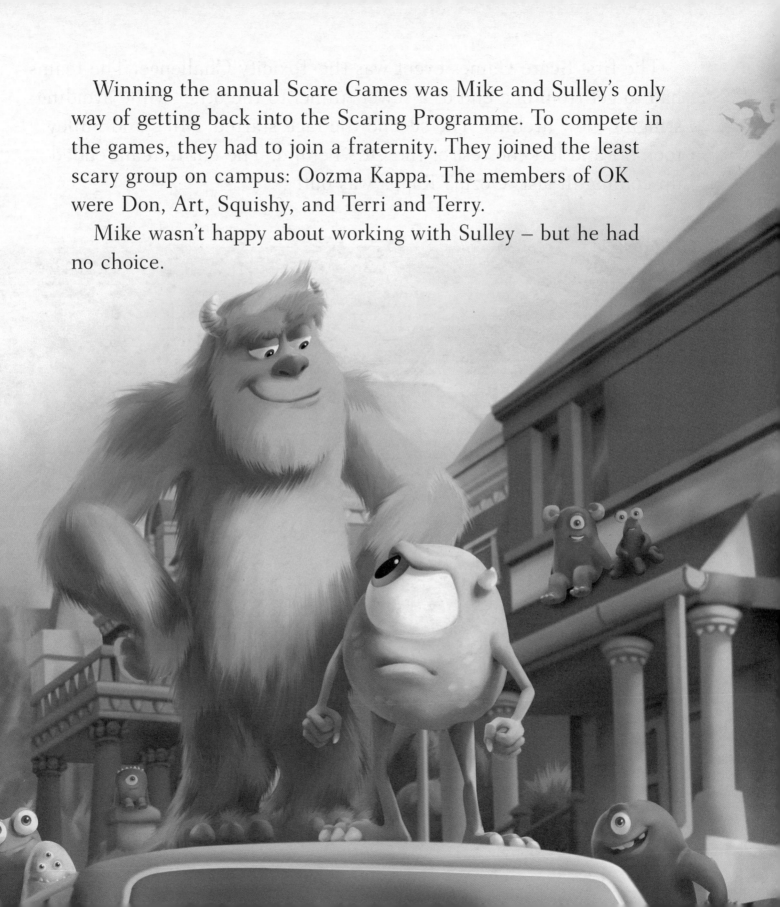

The first Scare Games event was the Toxicity Challenge. The teams had to get from one end of a sewer tunnel to the other while avoiding stinging glow urchins. The second the race started, Mike and Sulley took off and left the rest of the OKs behind. The entire team ended up coming in last. Oozma Kappa was out!

Then, suddenly, one of the winning teams was disqualified for cheating. The OKs were back in!

The next day, the OKs showed Mike some of their talents, but Mike already had a plan. "From now on we are of one mind ... my mind," he said.

Sulley rolled his eyes. "You tell them what to do, but not me. Later coach," he muttered.

The second event, Avoid the Parent, took place in
the library. The teams had to capture their flag without
getting caught by the librarian! Even though
Sulley was no help to the team at all,
the OKs managed to take fourth place.
Squishy had grabbed the flag
and made it out of the library
without anyone noticing!

Just as the OKs were starting to feel confident the RORs made fun
of them. They told the OKs they'd never be real Scarers.

Mike decided to take everyone to Monsters, Inc. They sneaked
up onto the roof and looked down onto a scare floor. They saw that
Scarers came in all shapes and sizes. Everyone was inspired.

Mike and Sulley both admitted that they had been behaving badly.
They agreed they needed to start working together.

The following morning, Mike and Sulley bounded out of bed. They couldn't wait to begin training for the next Scare Games event! They packed up their gear, met up with the other OKs and headed off to campus.

Mike worked on getting the team in tip-top shape.
He taught them how to sneak into a bedroom, how to
drop to the floor and how to dodge teenagers.
In between drills, Mike got them to run on
the spot and practise their 'scary feet'.

The Oozma Kappas' training paid off. They passed the Don't Scare the Teen event and moved to the next round! Mike helped them to practise for the Hide and Sneak event. The OKs were so well prepared, they came in second.

They were heading to the finals!

Later, Sulley ran into Dean Hardscrabble.

"Tomorrow each of you must prove that you are undeniably scary and I know one of you is not," she said.

Sulley knew that she meant Mike. He didn't want to believe her, but he couldn't help but wonder if she was right.

The RORs and the OKs were going head-to-head in the final
Scare Games event. Each competitor had to perform a scare in a simulator.
    Mike was the last member of the OKs to perform his scare. He entered
the room, sneaked up to the bed, leapt out and roared! The robot child sat
bolt upright and screamed.

Mike's scare had given the OKs the highest score. They had won the Scare Games! Don, Terri and Terry, Squishy, Art and Sulley all surrounded Mike and lifted him on their shoulders. The entire amphitheatre burst into cheers and applause.

"We're in the Scaring Programme!" Sulley cried.

But the moment didn't last long. Mike soon discovered that Sulley had rigged the controls on the simulator. Mike's difficulty level had been switched to 'easy'. He couldn't believe it!

"Well, what was I supposed to do?" Sulley blurted out. "Let the whole team fail because you don't have it?"

Mike was angry. He stormed off and stole a key to the Door Tech Lab, where students learned how to build doors to the human world. He put a scream can in place, powered up a door – and opened it! Alarms went off all over campus, sending Hardscrabble and her security guards racing to the lab.

Mike found himself in the wardrobe of a child's room. He crept out towards the sleeping child and ... ROARED!

The youngster sat up and smiled. "You look funny," she said.

Mike couldn't believe it. Suddenly, he realized he wasn't in a child's bedroom. He turned to look and saw that he was in a cabin full of kids!

Meanwhile, Sulley rushed to the lab. He slipped past security, ran through the door and went off to rescue Mike. He found him beside a lake in the camp grounds.

"I thought I could show everybody that Mike Wazowski is something special. But I'm just not," said Mike.

Sulley told Mike he wasn't much different. He had messed things up his entire life. "I'll never know how you feel, but you're not the only 'failure' here," he said.

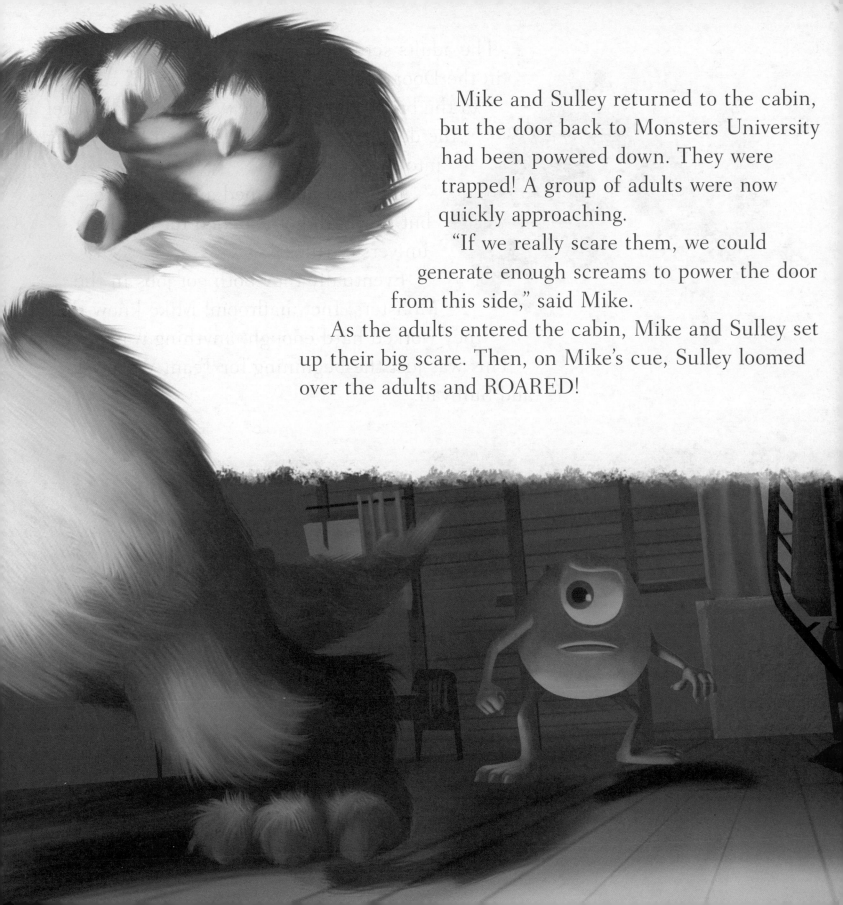

Mike and Sulley returned to the cabin, but the door back to Monsters University had been powered down. They were trapped! A group of adults were now quickly approaching.

"If we really scare them, we could generate enough screams to power the door from this side," said Mike.

As the adults entered the cabin, Mike and Sulley set up their big scare. Then, on Mike's cue, Sulley loomed over the adults and ROARED!

The adults screamed and ran for their lives. Back in the Door Tech Lab, the door's scream can filled to the brim! Hardscrabble watched in disbelief as the door exploded and Mike and Sulley blasted into the room.

They had performed an epic scare – but they still got expelled for breaking university rules.

Eventually they both got jobs in the Monsters, Inc. mailroom! Mike knew that if they worked hard enough, anything was possible. This was just the beginning for Team Wazowski and Sullivan.